The Spaghetti-Slurping Sewer Serpent

TAIL

SEPT 29 8AM

AUG 31

NOODLE!

DEC 31, 3PM

To: The Elk Library~
Wishing your readers
success with these
slippery letters!

Laura Ripes

by **Laura Ripes**   illustrated by **Aaron Zenz**

Marshall Cavendish Children

All rights reserved
Marshall Cavendish Corporation
99 White Plains Road
Tarrytown, NY 10591
www.marshallcavendish.us/kids

The illustrations are rendered in Prismacolor
colored pencil.
Book design by Vera Soki
Editor: Robin Benjamin
Printed in Malaysia (T)
First edition
10 9 8 7 6 5 4 3 2 1

 Marshall Cavendish
Children

Library of Congress Cataloging-in-Publication Data

Ripes, Laura.
The spaghetti-slurping sewer serpent / by Laura
Ripes ; illustrated by Aaron Zenz. — 1st ed.
p. cm.
Summary: Sammy Sanders sets out to prove that a
spaghetti-slurping serpent lives in his sewer.
ISBN 978-0-7614-6101-2 (hardcover) —
ISBN 978-0-7614-6102-9 (ebook)
[1. Snakes—Fiction. 2. Sewerage—Fiction. 3.
Spaghetti Fiction.] I. Zenz, Aaron, ill. II. Title.
PZ7.R4841Sp 2012   [E]—dc23   2011016406

To the one thing I love more than spaghetti—my family: Michael, Nikki, Ally, Jessie, CJ, and, of course, Charli.

A sincere thanks to Kristen Olds, the sensational intern who snatched Sammy Sanders from the slush pile, and to my skilled and savvy editor, Robin Benjamin, for her stupendous support.

—L.R.

For my Super Son Isaac

—A.Z.

Sammy Sanders can't sleep. He is 77 percent sure that a spaghetti-slurping serpent lives in his sewer.

After supper, when Mom scraped spaghetti into the sink, Sammy heard strange slurping sounds.

Slurp

Slurp

Slurp

The next day, Sammy sees spaghetti strands scattered across his street and a slimy sauce surrounding the sewer.

"There's no such thing as a sewer serpent," says his friend Scott Sullivan. "Sammy Sanders is a scaredy-cat!" snickers Steve Strauss.

Sammy decides he has to see this serpent for himself. So he and his sister, Sally, set out as spaghetti-slurping sewer serpent spies.

Sally spots a suspiciously slimy splatter. Sammy is certain this is the same sauce he's seen before!

Suddenly, Sally's sneakers skid on the sauce, and she stumbles into the sewer. She squeals as she slides out of sight.

Sammy shivers as he strains to see his sister. Scary thoughts swim in his head:

What if the sewer serpent spots Sally snooping?

What if Scott Sullivan and Steve Strauss see him sitting there sniveling?

Sammy has to snap out of it! He must save Sally! He shuts his eyes and shoves his arm into the sewer.

"Sally! Sally! Sally!" he shouts.

Something seizes his sleeve. He sure hopes it's Sally! With superhero strength, Sammy grabs it, swings his arm up, and sees . . .

. . . his stinky sister.

Sally says, "Sorry, Sammy, no spaghetti-slurping sewer serpents. Just a smelly, sludgy sewer."

Later, when Sally is sleeping, Sammy has a stupendous idea!

He snatches a salty snack for himself and a serving of saucy spaghetti.

Then he sneaks to his swing set and sits the spaghetti on the seat.

He sprints behind a shrub and waits.

Sammy struggles not to fall asleep.
Sadly, after a short seven minutes
and seventeen seconds, Sammy's
eyes slam shut.

As the stars shine down on the sewer cap, it shakes, then slowly shifts to the side.

A scaly, slimy sewer serpent
slips onto the street and slithers
to the Sanders' swing set.

The sewer serpent slithers up to the scrumptious spaghetti and slurps it from a spork while swinging on the Sanders' squeaky swing.

squeak

squeak

Slurp, Slurp . . .
SLURRRRP!

Sammy knows that sound! He wakes up and sees the serpent sniffing his salty snack.

Sammy stares at the
serpent. The serpent stares
at Sammy's snack.

Sammy sees there's only
one solution. . . .
   "Want to share?" he says.
The spaghetti-slurping
sewer serpent . . . smiles.
Sammy smiles, too.

The serpent swallows the salty snack and slithers back to the sewer.

He stops, spins around, and whispers to Sammy:

"Shhhhhh. Serpents are secret."

"My lips are sealed," says Sammy.

Then the serpent slips out of sight.

That night, Sammy Sanders sleeps soundly, 100 percent sure that a spaghetti-slurping serpent lives in his sewer!

SOLVED!